The Happy l
Christopher Tree

Ann Martin Rutland
Illustrated by Frank Martin

The Happy Life of Christopher Tree

Ann Martin Rutland
Illustrated by Frank Martin

ISBN 13: 978-1536874280
ISBN-10: 1536874280

Edited by Ann Martin Rutland and Frank Martin.

Interior and cover artwork by Frank Martin.
Background artwork by mabilal, https://www.fiverr.com/mabilal.

Cover design, interior design, and formatting by Diane Simmons Dill, *Right*Write Productions LLC, *www.facebook.com/rightwriteproductions*.

PRINTED IN THE UNITED STATES OF AMERICA.

Dedication

This book is dedicated to the memory of Geoffrey, and it is also written in honor of our other children and grandchildren.

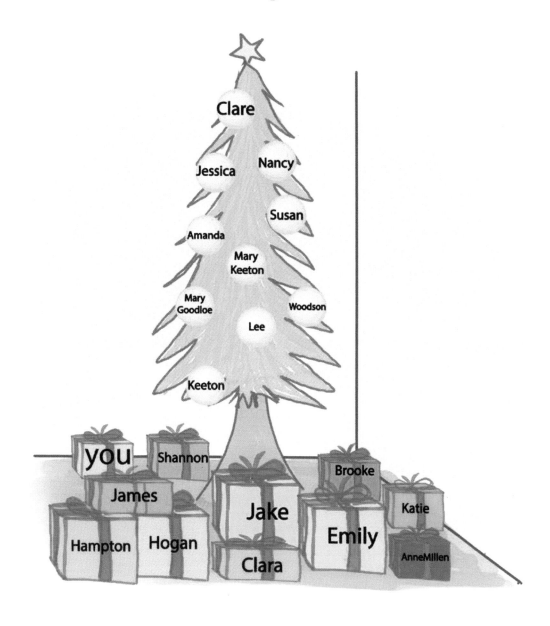

There was once
a little tree
whose name was
Christopher. He
came from a
long line of
Christmas Trees.

Christopher's greatest
wish was to be a
Christmas tree, too.

When he was very young, Christopher's mother told him the family secrets. He could think of nothing nicer than being gaily decorated to make a family happy at Christmas.

As he grew older, he noticed that every year just after the first snowfall, men would come into the forest, which was his home, to tie ribbons around certain trees.

When winter came, men brought axes and saws and took some of the trees away on big trucks. His mother said these were the trees that had been chosen to be Christmas Trees.

At first, Christopher thought...

Well, I'm only five feet tall. They will take me next year.

His roots grew deep, and he stood straight and tall. And he grew. He was six feet tall, then seven and eight feet.

Still, there was no red ribbon. The men merely glanced at him and went on to mark his brothers and sisters and cousins.

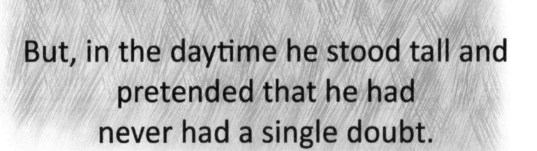

Sometimes, Christopher drooped at night, when the other trees weren't looking.

But, in the daytime he stood tall and pretended that he had never had a single doubt.

He knew just what to do to grow stronger and straighter.

He must take his vitamins, eat the right diet and always remember to stand straight and tall so his head would reach for the stars.

It was not many
years before
Christopher grew
tall enough
for the men to
notice him.

Or so he thought!
But each year the men walked right past.
There were no red ribbons for him!

Christopher had failed to achieve his only desire.

The little trees thought he was silly to keep taking vitamins and watching his diet when it didn't do a bit of good.

Christopher remembered his mother's advice to never become discouraged. She had reminded him every day that he should never give up hope. Maybe the next year he would be chosen, and Christopher kept hoping.

During his long life, he had seen many trees marked with red ribbons and loaded onto the huge trucks to be carried away for Christmas. He was sure that he would someday be chosen.

Many, many years passed, and Christopher was a tremendous tree. He was the largest tree in the forest. He was taller than his father and mother had been when they became Christmas Trees.

Christopher was 30 feet tall, and his lower branches spread long and strong from the trunk in all directions. He was surrounded by his children and grandchildren.

Christopher was so tall and

had been reaching for the

stars for so long that he

thought surely   he would

bump his head   on one if

he was not   chosen

before long!

Then one gloriously happy day just after the first snow, the men came again. These were not the same men who had come when he was little. Those men had become too old to come to the forest; these men were their great-grandsons.

This day the men came right up to Christopher. And, he heard them say, "Great-Grandpa was right. This is the most beautiful tree. See how straight he is and how very tall. There are no bare spots between his limbs, and he is so broad. He is just right. Everyone will be pleased."

The men brought in a big truck with the tallest ladder attached to it and backed it right up next to Christopher.

THEN THE MEN TIED A HUGE
RED RIBBON AROUND HIS TREE TOP!

Soon the men came with axes and saws
and began to cut   Christopher down.
Oh, what a happy   day!

As the buzz saws buzzed, Christopher sang...

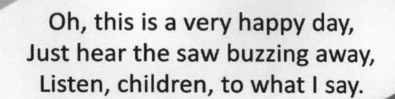

Oh, this is a very happy day,
Just hear the saw buzzing away,
Listen, children, to what I say.

Keep your roots where they belong.
Point your head at the starry throng.
Dream in your heart all day long.

No matter the odds with which you cope,
Don't be a quitter and sit and mope.
Never give up. Keep your hope.
HOPE, HOPE, HOPE!

As all of his friends shouted their blessings, he answered with happy good-byes.

The men put Christopher on a huge truck. He was so big he had the whole truck to himself.

He rode a long, long way through country that was new and strange to him.

Finally, they stopped. Some nearby trees told Christopher he was in a city, where many people lived.

The truck went to a lovely place in the center of the city that looked more like his home. He asked other trees where he was, and they said he was in the city park.

Christopher didn't understand why he was in this place rather than a home. The trees told him that he, Christopher Tree, had been chosen to be THE Christmas Tree for the whole city—not for just one family. He was much too large for a house.

Christopher was put in the center of the park, and the people decorated him. First came the lights, then the ornaments, and what large fine ornaments they were, and then came the tinsel!

Everything was placed just so. He was the most beautiful tree imaginable.

The night of the tree lighting, there was a parade. Santa Claus was there, and all the children of the city were there.

The parade came right up to Christopher and stopped. Santa touched a switch.

The beautiful lights blazed. Everyone in the crowd gasped at the wonderful sight. The children noticed first, and then their parents saw. The tree seemed to be smiling. And, he was!

Christopher made a whole city's Christmas happy. Then he had another surprise. After the holidays, he was loaded onto the big truck again and taken to a lumber mill.

There, Christopher's wood, along with wood from other trees, was used to make boards for sandboxes, swing sets, doll houses, toys, and all kinds of other wonderful things.

There were park benches to encircle next year's Christmas tree so grandmothers and grandfathers could enjoy the celebration.

And so it happened that Christopher Tree got his wish to be a Christmas Tree. It had never dawned on him that he would get so much happiness from giving himself to provide joy to others!

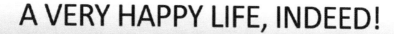

A VERY HAPPY LIFE, INDEED!

BE SURE TO LOOK FOR
CHRISTOPHER IN YOUR TOWN!

Merry Christmas!

The next two pages are here for you to color as you wish!

A Note From the Author

Thank you for reading my book! I sincerely hope you and your child enjoyed it. My goal in writing the book was to encourage children to persevere and to always believe they can do anything they want to do.

If you enjoyed the book, may I ask a special favor of you? Please take just a moment to go to Amazon.com and leave a review. I would truly appreciate it.

Many thanks and blessings,
Ann

About the Author and Illustrator

Ann Martin Rutland and her brother Frank Martin were born in Gadsden, Alabama, where they graduated from Gadsden High School in the 1950s. Ann graduated from Randolph Macon Woman's College, majoring in Political Science. She went on to serve others as a home executive and community volunteer. After marrying her extremely generous and supportive husband, she moved to Birmingham, Alabama, where she still lives. Ann and her husband have four daughters and nine grandchildren. Frank graduated from Vanderbilt and Harvard Law School and practiced law in Washington, DC. After retirement, he and his lovely wife now live in Charleston, West Virginia, and Magnolia Springs, Alabama. They have two sons and a daughter and four grandchildren.

Ann told this story to her four daughters as they were traveling to Gadsden to have Thanksgiving dinner with Grandmother and Pops. The youngest daughter was about three. She is now in her forties, so this is a rather old story. Ann says: "Never do anything in a hurry."

With the education Ann and her brother received, she feels that readers might expect something more erudite, but the story of this little tree tells all about striving and achieving one's dreams. Though the story is a simple one, it conveys profound principles that can be followed for a lifetime.

Ann wrote the story and Frank sketched all the images in *The Happy Life of Christopher Tree*, without which the book would be very dull indeed!

Enjoy the Book
and
MERRY CHRISTMAS!